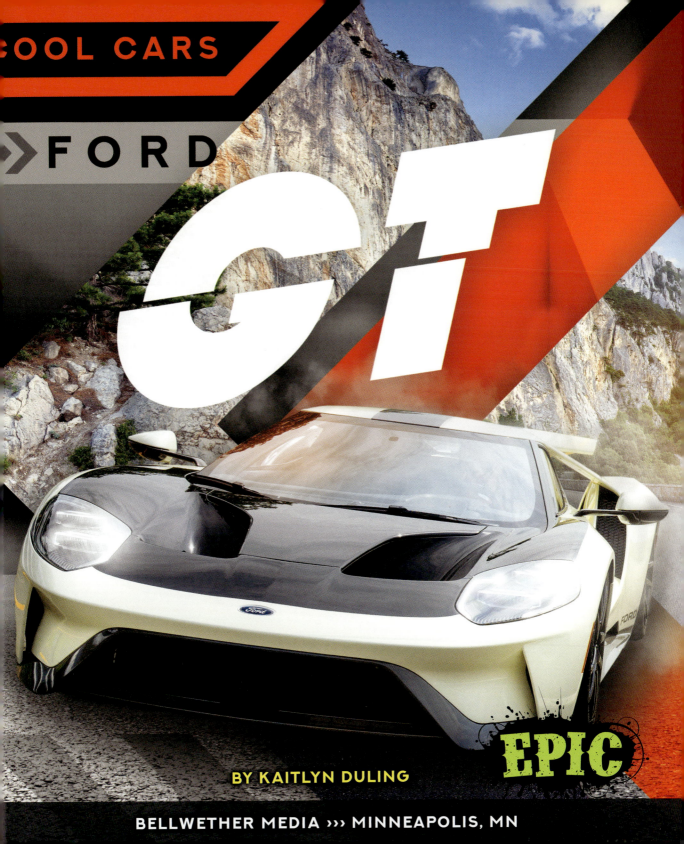

COOL CARS

FORD GT

BY KAITLYN DULING

EPIC

BELLWETHER MEDIA ››› MINNEAPOLIS, MN

EPIC BOOKS are no ordinary books. They burst with intense action, high-speed heroics, and shadows of the unknown. Are you ready for an Epic adventure?

This edition first published in 2023 by Bellwether Media, Inc.

No part of this publication may be reproduced in whole or in part without written permission of the publisher. For information regarding permission, write to Bellwether Media, Inc., Attention: Permissions Department, 6012 Blue Circle Drive, Minnetonka, MN 55343.

Library of Congress Cataloging-in-Publication Data

LC record for Ford GT available at: https://lccn.loc.gov/2022044258

Text copyright © 2023 by Bellwether Media, Inc. EPIC and associated logos are trademarks and/or registered trademarks of Bellwether Media, Inc.

Editor: Rachael Barnes   Designer: Jeffrey Kollock

Printed in the United States of America, North Mankato, MN

TABLE OF CONTENTS

MADE TO RACE	4
ALL ABOUT THE GT	6
PARTS OF THE GT	12
THE GT'S FUTURE	20
GLOSSARY	22
TO LEARN MORE	23
INDEX	24

MADE TO RACE

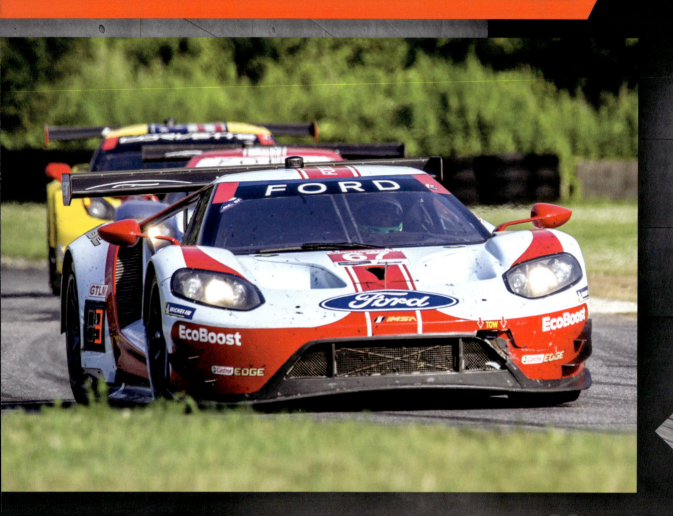

Cars race around the track. The Ford GT zooms ahead of the group.

A car charges across the finish line. The flag waves. The GT wins!

ALL ABOUT THE GT ≫

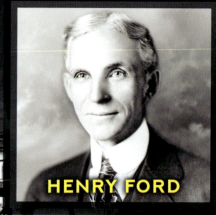
HENRY FORD

FORD MOTOR COMPANY IN 1913

The Ford GT is a car made by the Ford Motor Company. Henry Ford started the company in 1903.

The first GT came out in 1964. It won the **24 Hours of Le Mans** four years in a row!

WHAT ABOUT THE 40?

The first GT was called the GT40. The number is for the 40 inches (102 centimeters) the car stood off the ground.

GT40 AT LE MANS, 1965

Ford stopped making the first GT in 1969. But a new **model** came out in 2005. The latest GT released in 2017. Each GT model is faster than the last. They all look **retro**!

2017 GT

FORD GT BASICS

YEAR FIRST MADE — 1964

COST — starts around $500,000

HOW MANY MADE — 1,350 from 2017 to 2022

FEATURES

teardrop shape

rear spoiler

carbon-fiber body

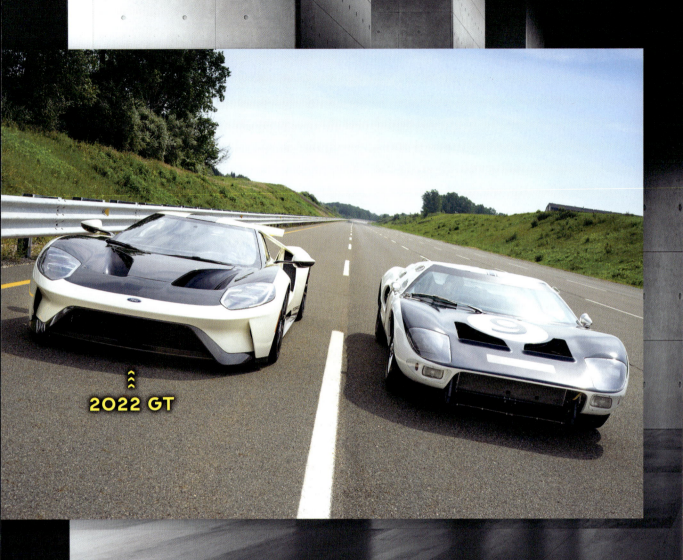

2022 GT

The most recent GT can reach 216 miles (348 kilometers) per hour. It is Ford's fastest car yet!

PARTS OF THE GT »

The GT has a **V6 engine** with **turbochargers**. This small engine is mighty. It can reach 60 miles (97 kilometers) per hour in 3 seconds.

A seven-speed **automatic transmission** sends power to the rear wheels.

🔧 ENGINE SPECS

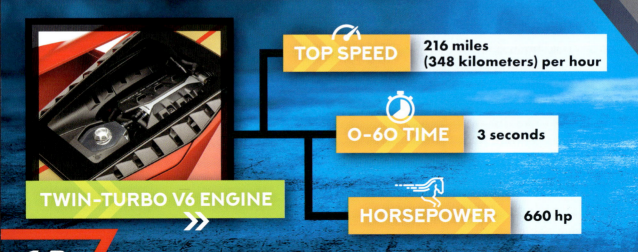

TWIN-TURBO V6 ENGINE »

TOP SPEED	216 miles (348 kilometers) per hour
0-60 TIME	3 seconds
HORSEPOWER	660 hp

In Track Mode, the car drops low for racing. Its **suspension system** helps it speed around the track.

SUSPENSION SYSTEM

SPOILER

AS SEEN IN
The 2019 film *Ford v Ferrari* tells the story of the 1966 24 Hours of Le Mans race. The Ford GT beat the Ferrari 275 GTB/C by nearly 400 miles (644 kilometers)!

The GT has a moveable **spoiler**. It can tip up to slow the car down!

> The GT is famous for its teardrop shape. It has **buttresses**. These make the car more **aerodynamic**.

BUTTRESS

SIZE CHART

WIDTH 78.9 inches (200.4 centimeters)

The GT is built for speed! Its body is made of lightweight **carbon fiber**.

CARBON FIBER

HEIGHT 43.7 inches (110.9 centimeters)

LENGTH 187.5 inches (476.3 centimeters)

17

Doors open upwards on both sides of this **coupe**.

Inside, the GT looks like a race car. Its two seats are fixed to the floor. Many controls are on the steering wheel.

THE GT'S FUTURE ≫

In 2022, Ford stopped making GTs. But racing fans hope to see another GT someday. Ford still makes other race cars, including the Mustang GT3. No matter what, Ford will keep crossing the finish line!

A FAMOUS THROWBACK

Ford made a small group of special GTs in 2022. They look like the 1960s GT race cars! The GT Holman Moody Heritage Edition honors the 1966 race car.

GT HOLMAN MOODY HERITAGE EDITION

GLOSSARY

24 Hours of Le Mans—a famous sports car race in France; the winner is the car that drives the farthest distance in 24 hours.

aerodynamic—able to move through air easily

automatic transmission—a car system that shifts gears for the driver

buttresses—tunnels that let air pass through them; the buttresses on the Ford GT are near the rear wheels.

carbon fiber—a strong, lightweight material used to strengthen things

coupe—a car with a hard roof and two doors

model—a specific kind of car

retro—related to past styles or looks

spoiler—a part on the back of a car that helps it grip the road

suspension system—a series of parts that help a car grip the road and move more smoothly over bumps

turbochargers—engine parts that force high-pressure air into the engine to create extra power

V6 engine—an engine with 6 cylinders arranged in the shape of a "V"

TO LEARN MORE

AT THE LIBRARY

Hamilton, S.L. *The World's Fastest Cars.* Minneapolis, Minn.: Abdo Publishing, 2020.

Labrecque, Ellen. *Ford GT.* Minneapolis, Minn.: Kaleidoscope, 2020.

Sommer, Nathan. *Ferrari F8 Tributo.* Minneapolis, Minn.: Bellwether Media, 2023.

ON THE WEB

FACTSURFER

Factsurfer.com gives you a safe, fun way to find more information.

1. Go to www.factsurfer.com.

2. Enter "Ford GT" into the search box and click 🔍.

3. Select your book cover to see a list of related content.

INDEX

24 Hours of Le Mans, 7, 15
aerodynamic, 16
automatic transmission, 12
basics, 9
body, 16, 17
buttresses, 16
carbon fiber, 17
cost, 11
coupe, 18
doors, 18
engine, 12
engine specs, 12
Ford, Henry, 6
Ford Motor Company, 6, 8, 10, 11, 20, 21
Ford v Ferrari, 15
history, 6, 7, 8, 15, 20, 21
inside, 19
models, 8, 11, 20, 21

name, 7
Ontario, Canada, 11
racing, 4, 7, 14, 15, 19, 20, 21
seats, 19
size chart, 16–17
speed, 4, 8, 10, 12, 14, 17
spoiler, 15
steering wheel, 19
suspension system, 14
Track Mode, 14
turbochargers, 12

The images in this book are reproduced through the courtesy of: Ford, front cover, pp. 3, 6, 7, 8, 9, 10, 11, 12, 13, 14, 15, 16, 17, 18, 19, 20, 21; Brian Cleary, pp. 4, 5; Composite_Carbonman, p. 17.